I AM THE THORN

Phyllis Roberts

with Illustration by Amari Lange

WORKBOOK PRESS LLC
187 E Warm Springs Rd,
Suite B285, Las Vegas, NV 89119, USA

Website: https://workbookpress.com/
Hotline: 1-888-818-4856
Email: admin@workbookpress.com

Ordering Information:
Quantity sales. Special discounts are available on quantity purchases by corporations, associations, and others.
For details, contact the publisher at the address above.

ISBN-13:   978-1-953839-32-9 (Paperback Version)
                    978-1-957618-31-9 (Digital Version)

REV. DATE: 31/05/2022

I AM THE Thorn

Illustrated by

Amari Lange

Dedicated to all who feel unloved

and unaccepted by society,

for those who don't

consider themselves beautiful...
Dedicated to those who look in the
mirror and cry...

For those who hide in the darkness...

For all who need to be loved...

For all who need a loving touch...

You are loved and I dedicate this book

To you...this dedication dictated to me

by my "Master and God" who loved me
also an unlovable!

This is my story..."I am a Thorn";
everyone who sees me thinks I am
a curse!

This is what... I always thought...

Why was I created like this?

What is it that I have done, to be a
curse to everyone?

CURSE
CURSE
SIN
CURSE
CURSE
CURSE
CURSE
CURSE

Those who saw me in the thorn patch avoided me

I was spit upon as if I were a disturbance to their life.

Why was I so hated? Is it my payment for the pain that my very existence in this world caused someone?

Even the animals stayed away from me,

the birds made no nest in my branches

Only webs from spiders, which stung others, lived with me

Because of THIS, it made me seem worse, if that was at all possible!

CURSE
CUR
CURSE

There was a man they called a prophet
who was traveling down my road...

He looked at me and His look seemed to
reach out TO me and INTO me

I felt something that I have never felt
before...I think its love!

I longed to touch him and feel his love
deeply!

Then He smiled at me and did
something odd...

He talked to someone who wasn't
there...

The people said it was called a "prayer"

I couldn't understand but I felt
something peaceful inside...

This peace seemed to make me feel
better and lifted my focus!

SE
N
LOVE

Then...I no longer questioned my life
and I felt peace inside my own surroundings

I began to see the beauty in the web
that the spider spun on my branch,
how beautiful it was in the morning
with the dew sitting on it's intricate
design!

I began to feel the sun that allowed
me to grow strong!

So I drank in its light and grew
strong and powerful!

If my purpose was to grow strong I
would have to wait to experience my use
when my time came... I learned to <u>BE!</u>

One day a soldier came to my branch...

I looked right into his mean face and felt his anger, it frightened me...

As he contorted with rage he pulled on my branch!

Then he slashed off the branch that I was a part of, and I felt the death of my existence, my life began to drain away and darkness fell UPON me!

I don't know how long it took but
All at once the darkness became
light and I experienced something amazing...

I felt something that I had never
felt before

It was the touch of someone's skin!

It was the wetness of blood...it was
NEW LIFE!

I had somehow been placed on the
prophet's forehead !

I was pushed deeply into His skin

My wish...and my curse turned into
a blessing because my creator gave
me my desire

Who was this Seer who carried
life inside of Him?

Who was this prophet who could
resurrect me from my death?

How could I be given this experience
when I was the one who maimed and hurt Him?

He gave me the only love I had ever
felt!

I asked myself, "Will I again become a curse?'

I then felt like I was put on the
earth only to fulfill this purpose...so

Who was I to question it?

CURSE
CURSE
SIN
CURSE
CURSE
CUR

They hung him high on a dead tree!

From my new vantage point, I saw things
I had never seen before!

I saw many people... and they too
appeared as thorns to me!

I saw things differently from that place,
and I felt love for them because I was in
HIM!

Then something amazing happened
again...

Darkness fell on the earth, the sun
darkened and the earth moved...

Men who were cursing him ran in fear
and hid!

We both hung there for a long time...then
He said...

IT IS FINISHED!

All creation and all existence cried
because of His pain

Then I realized **HE** WAS MY CREATOR!

ALL CREATION WATCHED AND FEARED
HIS DEATH...

HOW CAN WE EXIST ANY LONGER NOW
WITHOUT HIM?

HE IS OUR LIFE!!!!

It is Finished!

Then they took us down from the dead tree they hung him on...

The men who took him down, gently removed me from His forehead!

They laid my branch down and I fell off of the dead branch that pierced his head!

When they removed me from Him I felt life leaving me again!

Darkness once again fell on me!

I don't know how long I was on the ground...

But all of a sudden I saw light again!

I WAS at the base of the place where they hung Him on the dead tree... BUT...

I had changed...I had become a fragrant flowering bush!

They called me the 'Rose of Sharon'

Everything about me had changed... I no longer saw things through a thorns existence but through an existence of beauty!

I now saw through my creator's eyes.

I now understand that the life that pulses through me is part of HIM!

Inside of me I carried the secret... I have to tell you now!!

He is as much alive today... as I am.. I live!

His life exists inside of me and inside of YOU TOO!

I no longer fear dying!

I await all of my CREATOR'S changes FOR ME!

I know that no one exists without a purpose we are put here by HIM...

Even when we feel like a curse!

No one exists without HIM ...His name is Jesus !

Jesus can
change you...

HIS LOVE
CHANGED ME!

"I Am The Thorn"
By Phyllis Roberts

I am a little thorn I'm watching from my darkened
home

I am a curse unto the world I can't hide, run or roam

I didn't think I had a use I was mad to be alive

I heard a prophet pass my home, when the light

seemed to arrive

What manner is this man whose smile is so deep and
pure

This man who changed my atmosphere and made me
feel secure

As I survey my surroundings that once seemed so
uninspired

I realize it is beautiful, and 'to live' is my desire

I see the spider spin his web and wonder how it's done

I see the light form on its strings when dew drops hit
the sun

How different colors hit the ground and give off their
gentle light

and I'm amazed at how it comes from high above my
sight

Then one amazing happening which seemed to be so
wrong

Happened on a special day when my life
became so strong

An evil soldier plucked my bough and my life
drained out of me

He placed me on the prophets head I became
alive and free

He hung him on a tree just like the fruit that
hangs to feed

and from that vantage point I knew I'd soon
become a seed

His blood was what I caused Him, yet His
blood had made me free

And from that high and lofty place, new faces
I did see

They seemed to appear so vicious, their
words pierced him deep inside

I knew it for my body had pierced inside his
head and I just had to cry

And all at once something happened it became
dark again

I realized that we both had died I thought
my end was hard and grim

I fell onto the ground, his blood watered my
exterior

then people stepped and drove me into the dirt and
the interior

it wasn't long that things began to strangely

happen inside of me

I felt myself expanding and broke through the
rocky ground to see

There was a transformation of a thorn with many
cares

I became a flowering bush my beauty brought me
loving stares

The Rose of Sharon was the name that mighty men
called me

And part of the Savior Jesus flowed deep inside of
me to see

A beauty to those passing, a smile would invade
their face

And happily I gave them gifts of flowers to
embrace

For I know now my purpose and I know now my call

Jesus wasn't a prophet but my Savior and loved me
through it all